The Mockingbird's Manual

~ BOOK ONE ~

By SETH MULLER

ILLUSTRATED BY BAHE WHITETHORNE, JR

SALINA BOOKSHELF,INC
MULTICULTURAL PUBLISHING

© 2009 Seth Muller
© 2009 Bahe Whitethorne, Jr.

Library of Congress Cataloging-in-Publication Data

Muller, Seth, 1973-
  Keepers of the WindClaw Chronicles : the Mockingbird's Manual / by Seth
Muller ; illustrated by Bahe Whitethorne, Jr. -- 1st ed.
      p. cm.
  Summary: After discovering that she can communicate with the birds, a
Navajo girl embarks on a mission to learn new ways of thinking from her
feathered friends and pass on the knowledge to her people.
  ISBN 978-1-893354-04-3 (pbk. : alk. paper) 1. Navajo Indians--Juvenile
fiction. [1. Navajo Indians--Fiction. 2. Indians of North America--Southwest,
New--Fiction. 3. Human-animal communication--Fiction. 4. Birds--Fiction.
5. Adventure and adventurers--Fiction. 6. Prophecies--Fiction. 7. Southwest,
New--Fiction.] I. Whitethorne, Bahe Jr., 1977- ill. II. Title.
  PZ7.M918453Ke 2009
  [Fic]--dc22

                                                          2009005591

                    Edited by Tayloe McConnell Dubay
                    Designed by Bahe Whitethorne, Jr.

                    Printed in the United States of America

                    First Printing, First Edition
                 12 11 10 09 08 07 06 10 9 8 7 6 5 4 3 2 1

  The paper used in this publication meets the minimum requirements of the
American National Standard for Information Sciences — Permanence of Paper
            for Printed Library Materials, ANSI Z39.48-1984.

                    Salina Bookshelf, Inc.
                    Flagstaff, Arizona 86004
                    www.salinabookshelf.com

~Table of Contents~

~*Part One*~
Ellie's Discovery

Chapter One

Unusual Find

Ellie Tsosie stood at the edges of a dry streambed, known as a wash. She wore her black hair in a thick braid that reached down to her waist. Her grandmother braided her hair that morning. She tugged and twisted until she reached the end. She tied it off with a blue silk bow.

Ellie Tsosie, pronounced "So-See," forgot to thank her grandmother. She wished she had remembered. For, in the early break of the Saturday spring day, she felt the wind move around her. She saw wind pick up the rusty-orange sand and dance it along a nearby ridge. *It looks like a spirit from the Earth,* she thought.

The wind caused Ellie's skirt to billow and sway around the bottom. Although Ellie usually wore jeans, she sometimes wore her blue skirt. She liked how it looked with her favorite yellow T-shirt.

She heard the wind more than she felt it. It sounded like a roar in the sky above her. It happened every spring. The wind beat the land near Ellie's home in Kaibito, pronounced Kie-Bi-Toe.

She, her grandmother and her brother Kyle all lived by a place known as Wind Rock, a 500-foot tall butte that Ellie used to gauge the season. In the winter, she watched for dustings of snow that sometimes fell on the top of it.

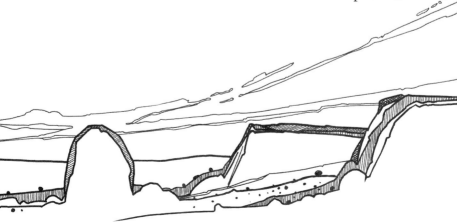

In the summer, when the sun tracked higher in the sky, the butte's shadow would nearly vanish. When storms came, Ellie sometimes saw clouds cling to the top of the butte.

On this day, the butte did not show any signs of snow or clouds. But Ellie sensed that the winds were swirling around it.

Ellie's grandmother taught her to like the wind. "Łahgo áhooníiłgo' áyóósin. T'áadoole'é nihaayiinííł," *It brings changes,* she told her. "It brings gifts." She also said this, as she said of many things: "The wind is an important part of our world."

Ellie still did not completely like the wind. When her hair was unbraided, the wind blew it in her face. Sometimes, it blew sand into her mouth, ears and nose. Once, it took part of the roof off of her grandmother's house.

She did enjoy the sound. And she liked

how, at times, it brought clouds and rain. She looked to the sky, but on this day she only saw thin and wispy clouds.

Ellie sat herself on a shelf of rock near the wash. In a land filled with good sitting rocks, she considered the shelf by the wash her favorite. It cradled her and let her dangle her feet.

A sage brush moved in the wind next to her. Ellie plucked a sprig from it. She rubbed the tiny leaves between her thumb and finger. She smelled the sage, which carried the aroma of every desert rain she could remember.

"Tł'óógó ch'inílyeedgo nizhónígo 'oo'áłiigíí banił hozhǫǫdo," *Go outside and enjoy the day,* Ellie's grandmother told her. She needed to go to the nearby town of Page, AZ to shop for groceries, along with Ellie's

Aunt Irene. Kyle went next door to her house, as he worked on an old motorcycle with their Uncle Rainey.

This left Ellie to wander, and to be alone. She sat on her favorite rock, unsure of what to do. She was bored, and she waited for something to happen aside from the gusts of wind.

Ellie looked up to the sky again. The clouds looked even thinner and the sky was mostly blue. She also noticed a dark speck moving high through the air.

She rubbed her eyes and looked a second time. She could still see the speck. She squinted, so much that she saw her own eyelashes.

It was a bird.

Once she saw it as a bird, she could not un-see it. The more she looked, the more she could make out its body and wings.

The bird struggled in the wind. It threw its wings up and down. It tried to keep steady in the gusts. Ellie watched.

Then it happened: an event that changed Ellie's day.

The wind caught the bird's wing so that it went straight up. Ellie saw something come out from under the wing. Was it feathers? It spun away from the bird and flipped and drifted toward the ground.

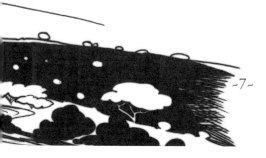

Ellie jumped from her sitting rock and walked into the dry streambed. She used her hand to shield the sun from her eyes. She watched the object sail and spin through the air until it reached the ground. It landed not far up the wash. Ellie ran to retrieve it.

It was a small book.

Ellie reached slowly to pick it up. She held it in both hands. It weighed less than she expected, as if the book itself were hollow. She studied the cover. It appeared to look like feathers from many birds, braided tightly together like her hair. The feathers were sealed under what looked like a heavy coat of wax.

She tilted the book from side to side. The sun reflected off of it. As she looked harder, she saw words that seemed to appear just for her. After a moment, she could read them.

The Mockingbird's Manual.

Ellie puzzled at this. She wondered if the

book transferred special abilities. She wanted to take it to her grandmother. She wanted to ask if she had seen anything like it. She wanted to know if the book would be safe to open.

Her grandmother, however, had left to buy groceries with Aunt Irene. She might not be back for three or four hours. Ellie wanted to ask her grandmother right away. She worried about all of those feathers. She wondered what they could mean and to what birds did the feathers belong.

Ellie fought her curiosity. She knew it best to wait for her grandmother. She squinted against the wind, which picked up grains of sand from the wash. She thought about the book and looked at it closer.

"Maybe I could take a peek inside," she whispered to herself. "It's just a book."

Ellie opened the book, which felt oddly

stiff in her hands. The pages did not shake in the wind like normal pages do. Instead, they turned rigid. They flexed to the wind.

Like wings, Ellie thought.

Ellie opened the book wide and the pages fell back to reveal a picture of a raven.

The raven appeared raised on the page, as if painted thick or in many layers. Without thinking, Ellie pressed her fingers to the raven.

Ellie's mouth sprang wide open.

A loud "Caw! Caw! Caw!" burst from her throat.

She threw the book to the ground and ran back to her sitting rock. Her hands shook and her throat hurt. The sound that came from her sounded exactly like a raven. It was more than a best imitation of a raven by a human.

It was as if a raven took over her voice.

Raven-Speak

Ellie sat on her rock and stared at the strange book, which she had dropped in the wash. Although the wind gusted and shook every plant, the lightweight book did not move.

Ellie wondered more about what her grandmother might say. Would she consider the book dangerous? It did carry a strong and undeniable gift. Might her grandmother believe the book too strong for her young granddaughter?

Or, might her grandmother celebrate the discovery? Maybe the manual was a gift of the wind. Her grandmother talked of windy days as wonderful ones. The wind spoke, she

would say. The wind carried stories.

Ellie put a hand to her throat. She wanted to touch the book again. She wanted to hear that sound leap from her. And, she wondered about something else.

"Could I speak to the ravens?" Ellie asked aloud, to the wind. Somehow she sensed the answer was yes.

With a mission in mind, Ellie suddenly leapt from her sitting rock and ran to the book. She picked it up with one hand. She ran up and out of the streambed, to a place where a fence followed a length of the dirt road by her house. On one of the fence posts, a raven perched himself.

The raven, *Gáagii* in Navajo, worked to keep his balance against the wind. He ruffled his black feathers. As Ellie approached, she guessed the raven to be one of the largest she had seen. If he stood next to her, he would reach her knees.

Ellie opened the book. She flipped to the page with the picture of the raven.

She pressed her hand to it.

"Caw! Caw! Caw!" The voice launched from her.

The raven turned to face Ellie. He stared at her for a moment with his black eyes. He tilted his head. Ellie opened her mouth a second time.

"Caw! Caw! Caw!" The sounds came out a little bit different this time. She followed it with a clicking sound that vibrated in her mouth. She remembered hearing ravens make the sound.

The raven lifted and flew toward Ellie. Her heart beat faster as he landed a few feet in front of her. Ellie stood still and kept her hand on the picture.

The raven made a similar clicking sound but Ellie heard it as more than that. She understood what he said.

"How did you learn to speak like a raven?" he asked.

Ellie did not move. She only stared at the raven with her hand pressed hard into the book.

"Well?" the raven prodded.

Ellie thought of what to say and spoke in the raven's language.

"I found a book." She held it up. "I think it's called *The Mockingbird's Manual*. It lets me speak like you."

The raven half-flapped his wings and bounced a step backward. He shook his head.

"I've never heard of such a thing. But I also have never heard a human speak to me like that."

Silence fell between them as Ellie thought of what to say. Unsure of how to respond, she introduced herself.

"My name is Ellie."

"What is a name?" the raven asked.

"It is what my family calls me and what other people call me." Ellie moved closer. She knelt down to be near the raven.

"In that case, my name is Stone."

"Why Stone?"

"When I was younger, I used to pick up stones with my beak. I would fly and drop them on animals below."

"Why would you do that?"

"I thought it was fun."

As Ellie and Stone talked, the scene of the two appeared strange. Had anyone walked past them, they only would have heard the clicks, gurgles and caws of raven-speak between the girl and the bird. They would not understand the conversation.

"Why do they call you Ellie?"

"It's just my name. Short for Ellen. I have a last name, too. It's Tsosie. I am Navajo. My clans are Dólii dine'é nishłį, dóó Dził ná'oodiłnii bá shíshchíín. My maternal clan is the Blue Bird People Clan and my paternal clan is The Turning Mountain Clan."

Ellie recited her clan names as an introduction so many times, it had become automatic. She seldom thought much of her clans these days, but she pondered her maternal clan: Blue Bird.

It dawned on Ellie to ask Stone an important question.

"What is it like to be a raven?"

Stone tilted his head to one side and blinked. The wind turned up some of his feathers.

"What is it like to be a human?" Stone asked back.

Ellie thought about the question. She realized it a tough one to answer. She knew Stone asked it back to her because of this.

"I don't know. That's a hard question to answer."

She thought for a few seconds. She asked, "What's the best part about being a raven?"

Stone unfolded and re-tucked his wings. He straightened his neck. "Well, of all of the birds in the world, we ravens are the most intelligent and the most resourceful."

"Really?"

"Oh, yes. We can live in the coldest lands and the hottest deserts. We never miss an opportunity for food. We are never wasteful."

Ellie thought about this virtue. She also thought of the times she saw ravens picking up garbage and rummaging through the odd treasures that collected in Uncle Rainey's truck bed.

"What's the best part about being a human?" Stone asked.

Ellie did not have an answer at first. She thought for a good minute.

"I don't know, really."

The raven and Ellie faced each other in the wind. She wished she could find a better answer.

"I have to go," Stone said finally. "I have much to do today. I also plan to meet friends on the other side of Wind Rock."

"Okay, then," Ellie said. "It was nice to talk to you."

"Interesting for sure." Stone nodded. He turned and took flight. He flew beyond the fence line and up into the sky until he looked like a black dot to Ellie.

Chapter Three

Meeting Buzz

Ellie puzzled over her conversation with Stone. It ended before she asked all of the questions she wanted to ask. What was it like to fly? What was a day in the life of a raven like? How many raven friends did Stone have?

She promised to herself she would be more prepared for her next encounter.

She opened the book and flipped backward from the picture of the raven. The pages started to flex and roll on their own.

They stopped.

Ellie smiled at the picture of the tiny hummingbird,

dahiitxı̨hí, with its emerald green wings, red-colored throat and long beak. Two days earlier, she and her Aunt Irene mixed the sugar water by putting a cup of sugar into three cups of hot water. They put it into a hummingbird feeder, an upside down bottle attached to a base. The base has little perches for the holes, which are made to look like flowers.

The next day, Aunt Irene stopped by to visit. She told Ellie the first hummingbird had arrived.

Ellie closed the book with her finger on the hummingbird page. She ran to her aunt and uncle's house. Uncle Rainey and Kyle worked on the motorcycle out front. Both had dirtied their hands with oil. Engine parts covered a blue plastic sheet.

The two did not take much notice of Ellie. She stopped running and walked around the corner and to the back of the house.

Her heart beat fast from the run. She stopped to catch her breath. She reached back to grab her braided ponytail and pulled it over her shoulder. Sometimes, she liked to run her fingers along the tight braid her grandmother created. It helped her relax.

The hummingbird feeder hung from the eve of the roof. Ellie studied it and looked around for any signs of hummingbirds. She also listened for the chirps and wing beats of an incoming bird.

At first, nothing came.

Ellie sat on the ground and watched the sky. She wondered if the wind blew too strong for the hummingbirds. The winds calmed down somewhat, but they still stirred the sage and picked up sand in places.

Out of nowhere, Ellie heard the pulse of chirps. The sound moved all around her. Ellie squinted to spot the tiny bird in the air. She did not see it at first. She looked up at the hummingbird feeder and spotted the little creature, buzzing and not that much bigger than a bum-

blebee. It featured the same color of feathers and long beak Ellie saw in the book.

Ellie opened the manual and pressed her hand to the picture of the hummingbird.

A sharp trill burst out of her. The vibration of it tickled her throat. The hum-mingbird almost landed on one of the feeders' perches. Instead, he flew up and hov-ered within inches of Ellie's nose. He flew so close, Ellie nearly went cross-eyed looking at him.

"Did you just say something? Was that you? Huh? Huh? Huh? Did you just speak hummingbird? How did you do that? Huh? Huh? Huh?"

As the hummingbird trilled and the words came at lightning speed,

he darted and shifted in the air. "Hold on! Hold on! Hold on! I'll be right back."

The little bird zipped to the feeder and landed. He drank up the nectar through his needle like beak. He drank like this from flowers, too. He stopped and let out a short trill. Ellie heard it as, "Ahhh! That's the stuff!"

He flew back to the place inches from Ellie's face.

This time, Ellie prepared herself with questions. However, Buzz had a few of his own.

"So, how'd you learn to speak humming-bird? Huh? Huh? Huh? Do you have special powers? Do you? Do you? Do you?"

"No," Ellie replied. "I found a book called *The Mockingbird's Manual*. It lets me talk to birds."

The hummingbird flew backward six inches and looked down at the book. He saw the girl kept her hand pressed to a page with a picture of a hummingbird like him.

"Yeah, yeah, yeah. I've talked to a few

mockingbirds. Yes, yes, yes. Down south. Sure, sure, sure. Not too long ago. No, no, no."

"Do hummingbirds call you by anything?" Ellie asked.

"Um, um, um, I'm not so sure. The mockingbird, though, he kept calling me Buzz. Buzz! Buzz! Buzz!" the hummingbird replied.

Ellie smiled at the hummingbird's fast talk.

"Hold on! Hold on! Hold on!" Buzz flew back to the feeder. Ellie stood up and walked to the feeder where Buzz perched himself.

"I'll stand here so you can rest on the perch," Ellie said. "I want to ask you some questions."

"Sure! Sure! Sure!" Buzz said.

"What's the best thing about being a hummingbird?" She asked.

"Good question! Yeah! Yeah! Yeah!" Buzz flew off of the perch and circled around the feeder. He darted around in the air for a few seconds before landing again.

"The best thing about being a hummingbird is that you're always on the go. Go! Go! Go! Always moving and working and flying. Yeah! Yeah! Yeah! And you get to drink from flowers! Sure! Sure! Sure!"

Buzz never stood still, even on the perch. He kept rocking his head back and forth, as if doing a little dance.

He drank more nectar.

"What makes hummingbirds different from other birds?" Ellie asked.

"Watch this! Watch this!"

Buzz launched from his perch and shot straight up into the air. He trilled with bursts of excitement. All Ellie heard was, "Yeah! Yeah! Yeah! Yeah!" as Buzz rocketed upward in a perfect line. He did this against the wind that continued to blow.

To Ellie, he appeared the size of a speck way up in the sky.

Buzz stalled for a few seconds, hovering in one spot. Suddenly, he burst into flight, shooting straight down to the Earth. Ellie tingled with the thrill of the flight as Buzz rocketed toward her.

Two feet short of striking the ground, Buzz pulled out of the nosedive and shot right up to Ellie's eye level, inches from her face.

He turned and flew upward again. This time, he flew in a spiral. He began in a tight spiral that opened up bigger as he flew higher. Ellie clapped, excited to watch a bird fly so fast and with such skill.

Buzz flew down to the center of the invisible spiral he created and returned close to Ellie's face.

"What'd ya think? Huh? Huh? Huh?" Buzz asked.

"That was amazing!" Ellie replied.

"Thank you! Thank you! Thank you! I love to fly! Fast! Fast! Fast!" He sounded out of breath. "But I need more nectar now.

Flowers! Flowers! Flowers!"

"See you around!" Buzz chirped as he began to fly off. But, he forgot about the feeder. He turned back and drank from one of the perches. "Ahhh!" he said. Then, "Bye!"

He shot off into the sky and disappeared. Ellie did not even have a chance to introduce herself.

Chapter Four

The Sister Claw

Ellie did not know the exact time, but she expected her grandmother home soon. She nearly imagined the pickup truck barreling down the dirt road, kicking up the red dust carried off by the wind.

Ellie wanted to meet one more bird while she had the chance. The bird lived in a place not far from Wind Rock, where tumbled boulders rested near an open field.

On mornings when Ellie did not have to go to school after chores, she sometimes walked the dirt road to the place. She and her brother created skinny trails that went around the sandstone rocks to places where the red rock became the ground. Ellie knew it as "slickrock" and the kind of rock as Navajo sandstone.

Near this place, Ellie often spotted a red-tailed hawk, *'atseełtsoii*, circling the sky. It also perched on rocks and old telephone poles that stood next to the road.

Ellie tucked the manual into the waist-band of her skirt. She climbed up one of the boulders, careful not to break any of the flakes or bumps on the brittle rock.

Once at the top, she surveyed the sky for any sign of the red-tailed hawk. When she did not see one, she opened the manual to the picture of the hawk.

She placed her hand on it.

A loud screech tore from Ellie's throat and cut through the air. "Eeeeeeeeee-yaaaaaaa! Eeeeeeee-yaaaaaaaa!"

In the distance, somewhere behind Wind Rock, Ellie heard a screech in reply. She looked in the direction of the sound.

She noticed the hawk screech hurt her throat worse than the other two calls. She rubbed her throat with her hand as she swallowed. She winced her eyes against the pain.

She wondered if she could have a whole conversation with the hawk.

Suddenly, Ellie spotted a shadow racing across the ground toward her. She looked up and saw the hawk. It flew fast and dropped into a dive. It came straight for her.

Ellie kept her hand pressed tightly to the page with the hawk picture.

"Please! No!" Ellie cried out. The hawk
pulled out of its dive. It circled above her before it landed on the boulder. But the hawk
kept its distance from Ellie.

The hawk let out a screech. Ellie heard it as, "How did you learn to speak like a hawk?"

In the tone of the translated words, Ellie knew the hawk was a female. The thought of speaking to a woman hawk excited her.

Ellie raised the book with both hands, one on the page and one cradling the book's spine. Wind swirled around the two, but they remained still. Ellie became scared. She did not know what to say.

"So, you're a human dabbling in the realm of birds," the hawk finally said.

Ellie nodded, still unsure of what to say or ask.

The hawk let out shorter, quieter screeches. Ellie heard the words, "Tell me, what is so special about being human? I have always wanted to know."

Ellie had not prepared herself further to answer questions, only to ask them. "Well," she started, her voice a tiny squawk. "We are storytellers. We have cultures."

"What else?" the hawk asked. She lifted one of her claws and flexed it. She bobbed her head for a second, but her eyes remained locked on Ellie's face.

"We create art," Ellie offered. "And music. And we pass down tradition."

The hawk did not say anything for a moment. Ellie wondered if the hawk did not understand. She thought of an idea.

"Can I show you something?" Ellie asked, her throat almost too sore to continue. "It will help you understand."

"You may," the hawk responded, her voice firm.

Ellie tucked the manual away and climbed down from the boulder. The hawk took flight and circled.

Ellie walked to the west of Wind Rock. The dry streambed — the same one in which she found the manual — began there.

The water cut a notch in the stone, which made it a small canyon. Ellie heard people call it a "slot canyon," *ałts'óózígo bikoh.* She stepped to the mouth of the canyon and to the base of a rock wall near it. The hawk landed on a boulder.

"There," Ellie said. She kept one hand pressed to the hawk picture in the manual and held it with the other. She nodded to a dark spot on top of the red-rock wall. "Can you see what's in the rock?"

The hawk noticed, with her sharp vision, forms in the stone. She saw the vague shape of two people. She also saw a spiral. It made her think of the circles she turned in the sky. Along with the two people and the spiral, the hawk could see the form of a snake.

"Humans made them," Ellie said. "Hundreds of years ago. It would be like the ancestors of your ancestors leaving a message or a story for you to read."

The hawk stepped forward, delicately. She blinked as she studied the forms on the rock. She let out a small screech. "I see," she said. "Beautiful."

A silence fell between them. Ellie took the moment to ask her questions. "I would like to know what is so special about being a red-tailed hawk."

The hawk looked at Ellie, with eyes as sharp as lasers. "We are the hunters. Our senses are keen. We are strong and we take pride in ourselves. We are solitary and independent."

Ellie listened and nodded. She asked one more question. "Before I go, I wanted to ask: Do you have a name?"

"My name is the sound the wind makes when cut by my wings." She did not explain further. Ellie imagined how that might sound.

"Thank you for speaking with me," Ellie said. She introduced herself in Navajo, including her clan names.

The hawk bowed her head. She then took

to the air. Ellie closed the manual.

The hawk screeched as she flew away.

Chapter Five

The Mockingbird's Return

Ellie followed the cut of the dry stream-bed across the open land. It led her away from Wind Rock. She returned to her favorite sitting spot.

The wind kicked up sand around her, but she did not mind. Ellie focused on the stones and small, carved gullies along the wash.

After some time, Ellie passed along side Aunt Irene and Uncle Rainey's house. She arrived at her rock a few minutes after that.

Ellie looked to the place where she discovered *The Mockingbird's Manual.* Beyond the streambed from that place, she noticed a rustling of bushes. It looked different from the way the wind moved the bushes.

It looked more like some animal moved them.

Suddenly, a bird sprung up and flew into the wash. It had gray-brown feathers and white bars on its wings. Ellie knew this bird was the mockingbird, *zahalánii*. She knew he was looking for his manual.

For a second, Ellie thought to keep the manual for herself. She loved the power it gave her. She knew, however, it would be wrong to keep it. It did not belong to her. It belonged to the mockingbird.

Ellie opened the manual and searched for the picture of a mockingbird. She flipped through it one time and did not see it. She flipped backward through the manual, slower and more carefully. She still did not see it.

"How do I talk to this mockingbird if he's

not in his own manual?" Ellie asked herself quietly.

The bird flew around more wildly. It did not notice Ellie sitting on the rock, a short distance away.

The mockingbird took to the air and circled the sky. Ellie stood up, afraid the bird would fly too far away to hear her.

Out of frustration, Ellie placed four fingers in the book at one time to see what would happen. As she did this, she touched the pictures of the three birds — the raven, the hummingbird and the red-tailed hawk — all at the same time. Her fourth finger touched the first blank page of the book.

She opened her mouth.

A strange sound of all three birds' voices coming together launched from Ellie's throat. The sounds together made

Ellie think of the way a voice can mix with a guitar or flute, or the way laughter of many people can become one sound. The caws and the chirps and the screeches all weaved together.

The mockingbird heard it. It called back to the girl in the same blended voice of the birds. Ellie heard it as, "I'm coming!"

The mockingbird flew up to the girl and landed on a nearby rock.

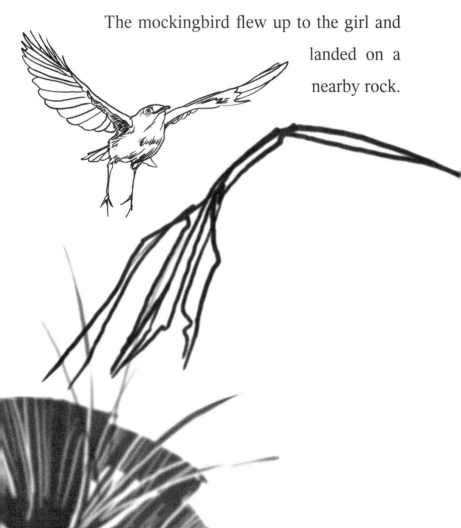

On hearing the voice, Ellie knew the bird to
be a girl, like her.

"You found my manual," she said in the
many-birded voice. "Thank you!"

Ellie kept her fingers on the pages. She
looked shy and a little scared. "I used the
manual," she told the mockingbird. "I talked
to other birds."

"Which birds were they?" she asked.

"I spoke to a raven, a hummingbird and a red-tailed hawk."

"Those are three very different birds," the mockingbird replied. She let out a sound like a laugh. "You must have learned a few things along the way."

"I did," Ellie said. "From each of them." She relaxed, as the mockingbird did not seem angry at her for using the book.

"That's the best thing about being a mockingbird," the bird said.

"What's that?" Ellie asked.

"Well," the mockingbird started in the many-birded voice, "we mockingbirds have the ability to talk to other birds in their language. By doing this, we learn of what makes them special. We learn of their values, and we try to make some of those values our own."

Ellie thought about this, as a girl who knew two languages and sometimes wanted to know more. "It must be nice," she said.

Ellie looked at the manual. She extended it to the mockingbird. The bird lifted her wing and the manual shrank and vanished beneath it.

Without the manual, Ellie could no longer speak to or understand the mockingbird. The two looked at each other for a moment, unable to speak or share. The mockingbird gave Ellie a sad look.

Slowly, the mockingbird lifted her wing and presented the manual back to Ellie. She smiled, and she took the book from the bird.

Ellie put four fingers onto the front page and the pages for the raven, hummingbird and red-tailed hawk. She spoke. "Thank you," she said with the voices of the birds.

"I realize I do not need the book as much

anymore, as I have learned to speak and understand most other birds. So, you may go, speak and learn from all of the birds you find."

The mockingbird prepared to fly, to battle the wind that still moved the sage. "Wait," Ellie said. "I never learned your name."

"I have a name," the mockingbird said. "I've always been known as Wide-Sky."

The mockingbird nodded to the manual. "Touch many pages in the manual and call my name. I'll come if I can."

"Thank you again," Ellie said.

"Thank you," the mockingbird responded. Then, she flew away.

Chapter Six

The Mesa

*A*s Ellie walked back home along the edge of the wash, she noticed the wind calmed. She moved past her aunt and uncle's house. Kyle and Uncle Rainey no longer worked on the motorcycle.

A rumbling sound came from the road. Ellie looked back to see the pickup truck. Aunt Irene and grandmother were returning from town and their trip to the grocery store. The sight of the approaching truck made Ellie nervous.

Ellie still wondered about how her grandmother would react when she showed her *The Mockingbird's Manual* and explained her day. Would her grandmother even believe her?

Would she see the book as good or bad? Ellie wondered if she should keep the manual a secret, at least for a few days.

The truck kicked up dust behind it as it traveled up the dirt road. Ellie looked into the distance, beyond the road itself. For the first time, she noticed something in the distant mesa. The afternoon sun did not hit the side of the mesa that faced Ellie's home, and it cast a shadow. The shadow and the dark rock face, together, appeared like a giant feather.

Ellie smiled at this. She ran home as the pickup truck neared. As she ran, she clutched *The Mockingbird's Manual* tightly to her chest.

~*Part Two*~
Seeking Knowledge

Chapter Seven

Tornado Dreams

awn erupted slowly. Sunlight streamed from the eastern horizon. It caught the shadow of everything and cast it long and thin.

The shadow of Ellie Tsosie stretched from where she sat, on her favorite sitting rock, to the rise of land past the streambed in front of her. Ellie's shadow mingled with the shadows of the sage plants.

With each passing minute, the sun became warmer on Ellie's back. The sky became brighter over Ellie's head. The breeze became steadier around Ellie's body. Her un-braided hair hung down to her waist, warmed in the sun and moved by the wind.

She sat alone with her thoughts.

She woke from a strange and terrible dream. In the dream, the nearby mountain known as Navajo Mountain — or *Naatsis'áán* in her native language — shook a storm from its back. The storm sent tornadoes dancing across the land, past the highway turnoff for Kaibito and down the road toward her house.

Without a minute to think, Ellie grabbed a rug her grandmother had woven. She stood out in the road. Her un-braided hair blew all around her face.

She yelled at the tornado, "No! No! No! No!" But it chugged toward her.

When she knew it was coming toward her and her house, she ran back inside and slammed the door shut. She hung the rug over the door. She watched her uncle hang a rug once, over the door to his hogan.

"For protection," he said. She decided to give it a chance.

She stared outside the living room window as the tornado twisted and squirmed its way up the road. It reached her yard and churned toward her house. The tornado ripped the door off of the house. The rug, barely suspended on two small nails, rippled in the wind but was not sucked out along with the door. Ellie let herself look outside one more time before she planned to hide. She gazed out as the tornado suddenly dispersed less than ten feet from the house.

Ellie woke from the dream scared. Because it was so early, she did not want to wake anyone — not her grandmother or her brother — to tell them about the dream.

Instead, she walked to her favorite rock, where she sat and wondered about the dream's meaning.

Her Uncle Rainey, in particular, did not like tornadoes or dust devils, which are the little whirlwinds that spin across the open land. "Bad news," he would always say. "Don't ever walk into one."

Ellie now looked to Navajo Mountain. Yesterday she had forgotten about it, as the weather that brought the wind covered it in clouds.

Was the mountain trying to warn her of a coming danger? Was she in danger already? Did she do something wrong that she needed to set right?

Ellie looked at *The Mockingbird's Manual*, which she came to think of as simply "the manual." Did she need to tell her grandmother about this now? Had she taken part in something she should have avoided?

On the other side of the streambed, she spotted a bird her Aunt Irene called a Stellar's Jay, *Joogí*, a type of blue jay. It perched itself in a juniper tree. It let out a loud screech, one that cut through the quiet morning air.

"Neeeeeeeeeee-yaaaaaaaaa! Neeeeeeeeeee-yaaaaaaaa!"

Ellie shook her head. "What an annoying sound," she said under her breath.

She looked at the manual and debated. Finally, she flipped through the manual until she found the picture of the Stellar's Jay.

She placed her hand on it.

Ellie opened her mouth and the screech ripped from her throat. "Neeeeeeeeeee-yaaaaaaaa! Neeeeeeeeeee-yaaaaaaaa! Neeeeeeeeeee-yaaaaaaaa!"

The call rang in her ears and sent throbbing pain through her head. Ellie wanted to toss the book to the ground.

"What is it now?" Ellie heard the words through the nasty call. She looked up to see the Stellar's Jay had flown over closer to her. It had landed in another juniper tree. He glanced in all directions, looking for the other jay he thought called for him.

Ellie opened her mouth again. "Hello there! Over here!" she said in the screechy call.

"What? What's going on?" the jay called back to her. "How is a human talking like a jay?"

Ellie grew tired of explaining. Still, she told him the story of how the mockingbird lost the manual. She told of how she found it. She talked of the raven, hummingbird and hawk and how she met them. The whole time, her jay-talk hurt her ears as much as her throat.

"My name is Ellen," she said as she struggled to talk in the jay's voice. "I have a last name, too. It's Tsosie. I am Navajo. My clans are Dólii Dine'é nishłį, and Dził ná'oodiłnii 'éíbá shíshchíín. My maternal clan is the Blue Bird People Clan and my paternal clan is The Turning Mountain Clan."

Ellie thought more about her mother's clan, Blue Bird People, as she stood before the Stellar's Jay.

"Blue Bird People, I see," the jay replied. "So, I expect you want to learn about Stellar's Jays while admiring my deep blue feathers."

"Sure," Ellie said in the screechy squawky language. "What's so special about being a Stellar's Jay?"

"Well," the jay said, ruffling his feathers, "we have a special connection to the juniper tree, or at least I do. Other jays have connections to other trees. They give us food and shelter, and, in return, we disperse their seeds so new trees can grow."

Ellie thought about this for a moment. She liked the idea that birds and trees could carry a strong connection. She liked the thought that the trees could be more than a place for birds to build their nests.

"Are Stellar's Jays the only bird with that kind of tree connection?" she asked.

The jay flustered. "Well, no, not really. But we jays are the only birds who know how to talk to trees. That's why we talk so loud. Trees are hard of hearing."

"Oh, I see," Ellie said.

"That's a joke, actually," the bird replied.

Ellie smiled.

"But I really can talk to trees," the jay noted.

"What do they tell you?" Ellie asked.

"They tell me to fly far with their seeds, to fly to the cliffs and remote places. They want me to scatter their babies to the spots where they can grow in the sun."

Ellie liked this. She liked to know she might learn from the trees — by talking to the jays.

"What else do they tell you?" Ellie asked.

"Well," the jay tilted his head back and forth as he thought, "they are old. Very old. Some of them are 600 years old. So, they share much wisdom."

"What kind of wisdom do they share?" she asked.

"See that one lone juniper tree down the streambed? She once told me trees are wise because they stay in one place. So, they know everything about one place, and they draw that place into them. It becomes part of their wood," the jay explained.

Suddenly, Ellie looked at the lone juniper tree differently. Still, she was confused about one thing.

"How can a tree tell you of all of this? They can't talk. They don't even have mouths," Ellie said to the jay with the screeches.

"I peck at the bark, and I feel it through the vibration in my claws. This is how I understand the tree," the jay said.

Ellie considered this, but she did not understand it. Still, she believed what the jay told her.

Without her asking further, the jay added, "We can fly, but we always return to the trees. We can get the wisdom that is rooted in the ground."

The jay noted, "I often call them 'the Elders.'"

With that last word, Ellie remembered something she had to do.

"Thank you, jay, for talking to me. But I have to go."

"Maybe we'll talk again soon," he said.

Ellie thought of her sore ears and throat. She smiled, "Maybe."

Chapter Eight

Un-keeping Secrets

*E*llie's grandmother stood outside the back of the house. She wore one of her long velvet skirts and a long-sleeved cotton shirt. She kept her hair coiled into a bun, but loose hair stood up in all directions.

With the rising sun behind her grandmother, Ellie thought her loose hair looked like a halo.

Before Ellie approached, she tucked the manual into the back of her waistband. She grew scared as she neared her grandmother, who had her hands on her hips. Ellie kept walking until she reached her grandmother.

"Hágóósh nísínílwod?" *Where did you run off to?* Ellie's grandmother asked her in Navajo.

"Níléégo'," *Over there,* Ellie said. She nodded her head in the direction of her favorite sitting rock.

"Is everything okay?" her grandmother asked.

"Kind of," Ellie said. "I just had a bad dream is all." Ellie felt the manual against her lower back. She worried her grandmother might see it.

"Well, you should tell me when you leave the house, so I don't worry." Ellie's grandmother straightened her back.

"Let's get inside. We have morning chores."

"Hágoshíí," *Okay,* Ellie said. She ran inside so her grandmother would not have a chance to see the manual. She walked fast through the house and into her room. She tucked the manual under her pillow.

She walked back into the living room, where her brother Kyle sat on the sofa. He ate his bowl of cereal in quick slurps. Ellie knew he wanted to get over to Uncle Rainey's to finish the motorcycle.

"How are things going over there?" Ellie asked.

"Good," Kyle said and nodded.

"Are you almost done?" she asked.

"Almost. A few more weekends, probably," he said.

He mumbled a goodbye to Ellie. He walked to the kitchen to drop off his bowl and headed out the back door.

Ellie's grandmother looked out from the kitchen and she shook her head. Then, she looked at Ellie. "Kodi bááh áshłeehgo shíká 'anil yeedgoísh bíighah?" *Can you come in here and help me make bread?*

"Sure," Ellie said. She still felt a little scared. Sometimes, her grandmother wanted to have a talk, one that had little to do with bread.

"While I warm some milk on the stove, you can mix the flour, salt and ash." Ellie's grandmother stuck out her chin to point to the counter.

Ellie quickly went to work. She used her bare hands, as she had watched her grandmother do for years. Ellie guessed that her grandmother used the wood ash for flavor. It came from an earlier time on the reservation. She imagined that her grandmother could find better ingredients at the store. She wondered if the ash came from a juniper tree her uncle recently cut down.

She remembered what the jay said about the lone juniper tree. She wondered if, when she ate the ash in the bread, she would eat some of the tree's wisdom.

"Ellie," her grandmother said. It startled her. "Is there anything that you want to tell me?"

Ellie's hands stopped. Her face went flush with fear. "Um, no," she finally said.

"Are you sure?" her grandmother asked.

Ellie turned to face her.

"Um, well," Ellie started. She tried to figure out a way to tell her grandmother the story. Could she tell it in a way she would get into less trouble?

Her grandmother waited. She finally said, "Yes." It prodded Ellie.

"See, I was out by the wash and I found this book, a picture book," Ellie started. In her head, the story began to fall into place. "I didn't know what it was at first, really. And, I picked it up."

Ellie took a breath. "The book was filled with all of these pictures of birds. So, I touched a picture in there, of a raven."

Ellie took a deeper breath. She exhaled before her final sentence. "When I did that,

I found I could … um … speak like a raven and understand what ravens said."

Ellie's grandmother slowly placed the rolling pin on the counter. She turned to wash her hands. She dried them on her apron and took the apron off.

She turned back to Ellie. "Let's go to the living room."

Her grandmother took a seat in the rocking chair Ellie's aunt and uncle gave to her a few years ago. It was her grandmother's first rocking chair.

"So, Ellie," her grandmother started as Ellie took a seat on the sofa. "Have you used this book to speak to birds?"

Ellie looked down at the floor, afraid to look at her grandmother.

"Um, a couple," she said.

She looked up. Her grandmother rocked steadily in her chair. She stared out the window.

"There is a story," Ellie's grandmother said after a moment. "I guess it is more like a prophecy. Do you know what a prophecy is?"

Ellie nodded.

"It's a prophecy that one day a girl of the Blue Bird People Clan would learn to speak to the birds," her grandmother said slowly. She looked from the window to Ellie.

"And the birds would teach her of new ways of thinking, to pass on to the Navajo and many other people. She would share this with the clan, who would take the message to places beyond. So we could better ourselves."

A wave of relief washed over Ellie. Not only was her grandmother not angry, but she also saw what was happening as important.

"Is that true?" Ellie asked, to be sure.

"Yes, as I remember," her grandmother said.

She stopped rocking and looked straight at Ellie. "Still, you should have told me sooner."

Ellie nodded. "I'm sorry."

"Just remember to not be afraid to let me know," her grandmother said. "Now, why don't you go outside? I'll finish the bread."

Ellie stood up, and her grandmother added, "T'áá nihít'éé nihił bééhózindo. Tsídii bits'ą́ą́ dóó 'íhoł'aahgo." *Let's keep this our secret, while you go out and learn from the birds.*

Chapter Nine

The Canyon Wall

*I*n the last year, Ellie reached an age where she was allowed to walk down the road to the far side of Wind Rock on her own. There, she often followed a dirt road, the kind her uncle called a "two-track" road. This meant the road only had two small lanes where the tires fit and grasses could grow up in the center.

Ellie reached the two-track road and walked in one of the two lanes up a hill. At the top, she sat on a sandy patch of ground,

where she took in a commanding view of Navajo Mountain.

She sat long enough to hear what she had heard many times before in the same spot. It went from a high note to a low note, like the sound of a plane dropping from the sky. But, it had a trill. It sounded like, "Peee-ewwww! Peee-ewwww! Peee-ewwww! Peee-ewwww! Peee-ewwww! Peee-ewwww!"

Quickly, Ellie pulled out the manual. She found the picture of the canyon wren, *tsénoł ch'ooshii*, with its mostly brown, speckled body and its white neck. "Peee-ewwww! Peee-ewwww! Peee-ewwww! Peee-ewwww! Peee-ewwww! Peee-ewwww!" tumbled from Ellie's mouth when she placed her hand on the picture.

Ellie liked the canyon wren call better than all of the others. The melody of it spun through her head. The sound felt like a beautiful spring day.

The canyon wren's call sounded off directly behind her. Ellie turned. She spotted the wren perched on a boulder. She heard the call as, "Was that you who called me?" Ellie heard a sense of surprise in the question.

Ellie, hand pressed hard on the page, turned all the way around to face the wren. "Yes, it was me who called you," she said, but in the melody of the wren. Because the call of the wren was naturally long, Ellie found her sentence longer than she

had thought it.

"How is it that a human like you can speak like me?" the wren asked.

Ellie, again tired of explaining, sighed. She told the wren the whole story. However, she enjoyed telling it in the wren-voice. It soothed her throat and her mind. She also told the canyon wren her name and her clan names.

Ellie continued. "So, I came here because I always loved your call. I loved the sound."

"Thank you so much. I like it, too," the wren responded.

"I like to ask all of the birds what makes being them special, like what makes being the kind of bird you are different from other birds?" Ellie asked.

"Well, as you know, canyon wrens are glorious singers," the wren said with a flourish. Ellie sensed the wren to be a woman.

She said it in a way that made Ellie smile.

"But, we also make the best use of our environment. We build our nests high in the cliff walls. We do this for protection. We understand about being prepared, building our nests in safe places, away from predators, floods and other dangers," the wren explained.

"Where is your nest?" Ellie asked.

"High on a face of rock just beyond those trees right there," she responded.

Ellie knew this place as the south face of Wind Rock.

"I built it in a place where the sun shines
on it in the winter but not in the summer," the
wren said.

Ellie heard of this. Last year, she went on
a class field trip to nearby ancient ruins. She
learned of how the sun tracked more in the
southern sky in the winter, so it hit south-
facing cliffs. In the summer, the sun moved

higher in the sky and gave south-facing cliffs more of a chance to be in shadow.

She was surprised this canyon wren showed the same thought in where she built her house. "You're a smart bird," Ellie said.

"Thank you for saying that, very kind," the wren said.

"One thing I forgot to ask you is whether you have a name," Ellie said suddenly. "Something I can call you."

The wren thought about it for a moment. In her melody, she said, "You can call me Lightsong."

Ellie stood and wiped off her pants. She pulled her long black hair around and over her shoulder. She had forgotten that it remained un-braided.

Ellie turned and looked downhill toward the road. Not far away, she saw her brother Kyle walking. He stepped off of the road, but walked in a direction that took him out farther from Ellie.

"Do you know who that is?" Lightsong asked.

"That is my brother, and his name is Kyle," she said.

"Why don't you call him over here?" the wren wondered.

"He cannot hear me. He has earphones in his ears and he's listening to music," Ellie explained, the song of the wren carrying out her words.

"What are you talking about?" Lightsong asked.

Ellie explained music, music players and earphones to the bird, and she noted how her brother listened to his music louder than most.

"So, he cannot hear the birds or the wind or anything else around him?" Lightsong asked.

"Nothing but the music in his ears," she said.

Lightsong struggled with this idea. Her world was one of sound. Not being able to hear another canyon wren calling or other birds would be difficult for her. She also would not hear her other favorite sounds, such as the wind or the rain.

Kyle walked until he disappeared behind a rise of land. He never heard his sister or the canyon wren and their unusual way of talking to each other in wren language.

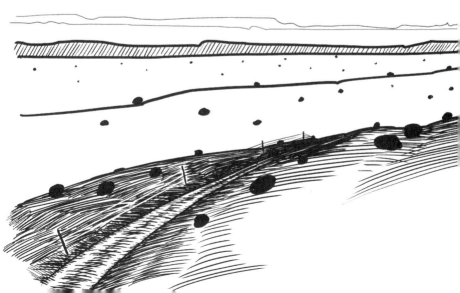

Ellie thought to tell the wren about how her brother seldom spoke in his Navajo language anymore, despite being scolded by his grandmother. And, she thought to mention how, a few years ago, they always played outside together. They climbed rocks, walked along the wash and flushed rabbits out of the bushes.

Ellie did not say any of this to Lightsong. She only said, "My brother is still a good person."

And, without thinking on it much, Ellie took her hand from the manual and closed it.

Chapter Ten

The Stone Reunion

When morning gave way to noon, Ellie noticed the day warmed fast. The spring day picked up hints of summer. Ellie already noticed a few tiny yellow wildflowers poking out along the wash.

In the last year, Ellie began to embrace the changing of seasons. She picked up on the sounds, smells and sights that came with each change.

Winter brought the smell of smoke in the air from her aunt and uncle's woodstove fires. Spring brought stronger smells of sage and the sight of flowering plants. Summer brought the smell of rain and sometimes the earthy smell of a flash flood with the afternoon storms.

In the fall,
Ellie heard the honks
of Canada geese as
they flew overhead.
They stopped over or
wintered at nearby Lake Powell, AZ.

Ellie tried to enjoy the sudden change in the weather. But her thoughts kept slipping back to her brother and her conversation with Lightsong.

So, he cannot hear the birds or the wind? Ellie remembered Lightsong's question. Was her brother blocking out too much of the world around him? Certainly, music was not bad. Ellie liked listening to music herself. But Kyle seemed to use music to block everything out.

Ellie walked along the two-track dirt road and back to the dirt road that ran past her house. After yesterday's cool winds, she found herself sweating a little. She wished her grandmother had braided her hair so she could be cooler.

In the distance, Ellie spotted a black form on top of a fencepost. As she moved closer to it, she saw it was a raven — a big one.

Ellie knew it must be Stone.

With her hand pressed to the page that pictured the raven, Ellie called out for him.

"Stone! Stone! Stone!"

The raven heard her call. He took flight from the fencepost toward Ellie. He landed on the ground near her feet.

"Hello again," Stone said to her. "What kind of exploring have you been up to?"

Ellie realized that Stone became the first bird she met. So, she listed off her other bird encounters to him, until she reached the canyon wren. Stone listened. He gazed at her steadily with his small black eyes.

She also told Stone about what her grandmother said, about the story of the bird-talker.

"She told me I should go out and learn something from the birds. She told me to bring back the knowledge and we could tell others."

"That's quite a mission," Stone said with clicks and caws.

Ellie kneeled along side of the road to talk further with Stone.

"Do you have knowledge to pass along to me?" Ellie asked the raven. "Something important?"

"I don't know," Stone replied. "I would have to think about it."

In an odd gesture, Stone turned and walked

away from Ellie. He left his claw prints in the sandy edge of the road. He suddenly turned and walked back to Ellie. When he reached her, he turned and walked away from her again.

"Are you pacing?" Ellie asked in raven-speak.

"Thinking," Stone replied with a single caw.

Ellie, still kneeling, leaned back and looked at the sky. It returned to a solid blue, bold and deep. It looked much different from the browns and reds of the baked-earth lands around Ellie's home.

Ellie imagined how open the sky must feel to a bird. *True home to the birds*, she thought.

Suddenly, without warning, Stone let out a loud caw.

"I have it!" he said.

"Have what?" Ellie asked.

"I know what knowledge to pass along to you," he said excitedly. "You'll have to follow me."

"Let's go," Ellie said. Stone took to the air and circled above Ellie, but moved the circle forward so Ellie knew which way to walk.

Chapter Eleven
A Circle Broken

Ellie followed Stone for nearly half-an-hour. They traveled west along the dirt road on which Ellie lived. She found it strange to see the land as she moved slowly across it. Normally, she watched it instead from riding in her uncle's pickup truck or in her aunt's car.

Stone turned off the road and Ellie followed on the ground, into the sand and sagebrush that covered the land. Ellie walked around the cacti and tumbleweeds, careful to avoid their sharp thorns. She and the raven neared a short mesa that stood north of Wind Rock.

She had never walked to the mesa. It had

no clear path to it and she had no reason to go. She did wonder, though, what she might find on top of the mesa. In the wide open country around her home, Ellie saw a number of interesting places in the distance that sparked her imagination.

An hour passed and Ellie still followed Stone. She began to worry about wandering so far from home and getting lost. She also did not have any water with her, and her mouth felt parched.

She pulled out the manual, and called up to Stone. "Caw! Caw! Caw! Prrr-raaa!" sprang from her. Stone heard it as "I'm tired and thirsty! How much farther?"

Stone called back, "Not far! Not far!"

He circled and turned in the direction of

the mesa. It had a short cliff, maybe 100 feet tall. At the base of the cliff, the land sloped at an angle. The sloped land was littered with rocks. Ellie wished she knew exactly where Stone was taking her. She hoped not to the top of the mesa.

"Caw! Caw! Caw! Ca-raw! Ca-raw! Raw! Raw!" Stone called down, but Ellie did not have the manual out. She placed her hand on the raven picture and called back with raven-speak.

"What was that?" she asked.

"Go up the slope! To the place where it stops at the cliff!" He called back.

Ellie listened to him. She began to climb, but the rocky slope made it difficult. For the first time she could remember, Ellie wished she could fly like a bird and not have to deal with climbing up to places.

Because of all of the tumbled rocks and

boulders and scratchy shrubs, Ellie struggled to find a path. Toward the top of the slope, Stone landed on a tall boulder right next to the cliff face. He appeared to wait for Ellie in the spot he wanted her to reach.

Ellie sighed. Her thirst nagged at her. She began to feel scared, wondering how she would make the walk back home without any water. *What was I thinking?* she thought to herself. She wondered if she might have gone a little crazy, following a raven around.

Slowly, Ellie picked her way up the rocks. Once or twice, she lost footing and slid back a few feet. A third time, she stepped on a loose rock and it flipped up and skinned her anklebone. "Ow!" she cried out, her voice echoing from the cliff face.

"Caw! Caw! Ca-wall!" Stone said. Ellie did not bother to take out the manual. She was sure he said, "You're almost there!"

Ellie came around a large boulder to find Stone perched himself only a short distance away. The slope became steeper. Ellie placed her hands on the ground for balance.

Out of breath, she plopped down on a rock roughly sitting height. She nearly fell off of it, dizzy from the ascent. She pulled out the manual, ready for Stone to speak.

"You made it!" he announced.

Ellie only nodded.

"When you are ready, I want you to walk to the base of the cliff behind me," Stone said with a series of clicks and gurgles. "You will see a dark stain on the wall where a spring used to flow. Look up from there."

Ellie nodded again. She wished the spring still flowed so she could get a drink.

She figured that if she passed out where she sat, no one would know where she was. Stone would know, but he would not be able to tell anyone. They would only hear frantic raven noise.

Finally, she stood, ready to find out why Stone brought her all this way, more than an hour's walk from her home, up the slope of a mesa.

"What is it?" Ellie asked in Stone's language.

"Go look," he said.

Ellie walked the last few feet to the true base of the cliff. She found the dark spot where the spring once flowed. She looked up.

There, she saw rock art. It was not pecked into the wall like the rock art Ellie knew. Instead, it looked as if someone painted it on. She learned about this in school, the difference between a "petroglyph" and a "pictograph." The first was pecked in the rock and the second was painted on the rock.

The rock art depicted four human forms, with their arms reaching up toward the sky. Above them, a bird-like figure was painted. Ellie marveled at the rock art. To the sides of the people and the birds, Ellie saw two forms of bighorn sheep.

She found it interesting that Stone knew of this site and brought her here. It was the reverse of what happened earlier, when Ellie showed the red-tailed hawk the rock art site.

"So," the raven started. "There is something you must know. You see, we ravens have stories from a time when ravens and people communicated and worked together."

"Really?" Ellie asked, her attention still on the rock art. She turned to Stone. "How is that?"

"Well, the ravens helped the hunters who used to live here. We ravens are intelligent animals, and we could fly high up in the air and find the animals they wanted to hunt. Then, we led the hunters to the animals. The hunters killed them for food, but they left some of the animal for us. Because we are scavengers, we eat all of the leftovers, so to speak."

Stone continued, "So, it was like this for a long time. The ravens worked with the hunters and became rewarded.

We communicated in certain ways, learned from each other and benefited from each other."

Ellie sat down again, still dizzy from the trek up the slope. But, she listened intensely.

"Then, one day, the hunters stopped hunting. People stopped needing the ravens. They found food in other ways, I guess. The circle was broken. We no longer benefited from one another."

Stone chortled. "We always thought that one day we might again communicate with humans."

~*Part Three*~
Bringing Balance

Chapter Twelve

A Tangled Wind

The temperature continued to rise through the afternoon. It turned more summer than spring. For the first time of the season, the ground began to heat. Rocks became warm to the touch.

Ellie walked across the open land, which offered no shade. She carried no water and no food. Stone flew slow circles above her. Ellie kept her eyes on the ground, where she watched his shadow turn around hers.

"If I die out here, you better not eat me," Ellie mumbled to Stone, but he did not hear.

She laughed. She thought it funny that a girl, wandering out in the desert alone, was being circled by a scavenging bird.

To anyone else, it might appear as if the raven waited for her to become lunch.

Sweat ran down Ellie's back. It also found its way into her eyes and made them sting. Still, Ellie kept walking. She looked up every so often in search of the road, but it hid in the hilly land.

Ellie was angry at herself for going so far without water, but she felt less scared the more she walked. She knew she was not far from the road. She found the footprints she made walking out and followed them back.

She approached an outcropping of rock she remembered passing earlier. She stopped to sit down. Stone drifted down from the sky and bounced and flapped into a landing.

A wave of dizziness swept through Ellie. Her mouth went dry and her legs turned sore. Ellie reached around and grabbed her hair. She tied it in one large knot, to get some of it off of her back.

Ellie looked toward Navajo Mountain, *Naatsis'áán*. It rose from the horizon. She could not help but want to visit the mountain, to see it close up.

As Ellie gazed out, she noticed something between her and *Naatsis'áán*. At first, it looked like a cloud of sand. But, as it moved closer to her, Ellie realized it was a dust devil.

A sweep of panic moved through her. The dust devil rose as a large column into the sky. The whirlwind was big enough around to cover a small house.

Ellie found it odd to see such a large dust devil on a day with little wind. This scared her even more.

Suddenly, Ellie wanted to get away. She began to run, although her legs were tired.

Stone, who distracted himself by pulling at blades of a dry clump of grass with his beak, heard Ellie dash away. He took off and followed her. He called out to her as she ran.

"Ca-caw! Caw! Ca-caw!"

Ellie pulled out the manual. She sandwiched her hand on the raven page. She squeezed on the cover with her other hand.

She called out to Stone in raven-speak.

"The dust devil!" she called out, almost breathless. "I'm scared!"

Stone called back. "Don't be! Watch this!"

Ellie stopped running and looked up.

Stone circled back to the dust devil, which closed in on Ellie. Her mouth began to quiver, as if she might cry.

She kept her eyes on Stone.

He flew into the dust devil.

"No!" Ellie cried out. She feared Stone might become affected by it.

She watched, helpless, as Stone's body spun circles inside the whirlwind. He struggled to stabilize himself.

Ellie wanted to turn and run, as the giant dust devil was seconds away from reaching her — but she could only watch.

Suddenly, Stone began to fly upright. He flew at an angle. He turned circles in the whirlwind and worked his way to the bottom.

Stone then did something that surprised Ellie. He quickly turned and flew clockwise, in the opposite direction of the churning dust devil. He flew fast, beating his wings as hard as he could.

Although Stone was only one raven, he somehow counteracted the giant whirlwind.

It broke up and scattered into light winds just before it reached Ellie.

A few small wisps of wind caught her hair, but the rest of the dust devil disappeared into the air of a calm day.

Chapter Thirteen

The Gifts Inside

llie sat on the ground and waited for her breathing to slow. Stone landed near her. He also breathed heavy. Neither was ready to talk. Ellie smiled at the raven.

After a few minutes, Ellie spoke to Stone in his language. "That was amazing. Thank you."

Stone cawed back to her. "Why were you so scared?"

"It reminded me of a bad dream I had last night, about tornadoes. Also, dust devils carry bad energy," she said.

"Well, maybe they do," Stone clicked. "But they sure are fun to fly into."

Ellie let out a small laugh.

She stood up to walk when a wave of shock rolled through her. Ellie, in all of her excitement, did not realize what had happened.

She had dropped the manual.

This meant she talked to Stone without using it.

Ellie looked to her left, where she spotted the manual, lying face up on the ground.

"Stone!" Ellie cried out in his language. "This is crazy!"

Ellie's caws and squawks echoed from the mesa in the distance.

It dawned on Ellie. Somehow, she absorbed the gifts from the manual — or learned along the way to speak in raven without knowing it.

"How weird is that?" she said, with different accents on her caws and clicks. She said the same words in English and in Navajo. She switched between the three languages, saying different things and marveling at the sounds.

Stone shook his head. He took off and circled in the direction of the road.

Ellie walked over to the manual. She picked it up and dusted the sand off of it.

Once she let herself calm down, Ellie began to walk again. She walked for ten minutes and finally reached the dirt road that led back to her house.

Stone landed and skipped and walked along side of her. Ellie knew she still had a long walk to go. She let out a sigh.

Ellie followed the edge of the road. She found its compacted dirt and rock easier for walking than the sand and loose rock of the open plain.

After a few minutes of walking the road, Ellie heard a rumble behind her. She turned to see dust kicked off the road in the distance. A truck cleared a small rise.

It was Uncle Rainey.

Ellie cawed up to Stone, who circled around her.

"You'd better go," Ellie told Stone in raven-speak. "My uncle is coming."

"Alright," Stone said. "Come and find me again, or I will find you."

"I will," Ellie called back.

Stone broke from his circle of flight and rose into the air. He flew in the direction of a nearby mesa. As Ellie watched him fly off, she tucked the manual into the back waistband of her skirt and covered it with her shirt.

A moment later, Uncle Rainey slowed his

truck along side of Ellie. He rolled down his window.

"Hey!" her uncle called out.

"Hey back!" Ellie called, though her voice sounded weaker than she expected.

Her uncle tilted his head to the passenger seat.

"Looks like you need a ride back," he said. "Hop in."

Ellie ran around the front of the truck. She opened the

passenger side door. It let out a squeak that hurt her ears. She jumped inside.

"Can I get some water?" Ellie asked. Uncle Rainey reached behind her seat. He pulled out an old orange juice jug he used to keep extra water in the truck.

Ellie unscrewed the cap. She tilted the jug to her mouth. Although the water was warm, she savored the joy of it. Her mouth and throat were no longer parched. Her lips were not dry. Ellie put the cap on the water jug and set it down by her feet. *I should never take water for granted*, Ellie thought.

Uncle Rainey nodded. He put the truck in gear and they headed home.

Chapter Fourteen

In Flight

ncle Rainey seldom spoke. Ellie thought of Aunt Irene as the talker of the two. It would not be unusual if Ellie and Uncle Rainey rode in silence for much of the ride back.

Still, Ellie wanted to talk. She wanted to tell her uncle about what happened.

She instead asked a question.

"Uncle, why do you think dust devils are bad?"

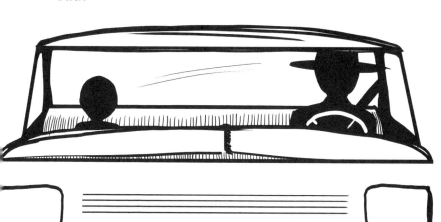

He smiled and scratched the whiskers on his chin. "Well, they sure are devils, aren't they? Hey!"

Ellie gave her uncle a dirty look, but held back a smile. As Kyle would say, Uncle Rainey was being cheesy.

"Seriously though," Ellie prodded.

"Well," her uncle started, scratching his chin again. "I always thought of them as imbalances in nature. Like, the wind is trying to turn in two directions to set something right again."

"Oh," Ellie said. She thought about it for a moment. She tried to figure out another question.

"What if," Ellie began to say. She stopped to make sure her question did not reveal any secrets. "What if a dust devil was coming toward you, but before it reached you, it vanished?"

"I don't know," Uncle Rainey shrugged. "I'd guess that something happened to fix the imbalance. To set things right again."

Ellie looked out of the truck's passenger window as the land rolled by. A feeling of relief moved through her. She realized that her new friendship with Stone might be offsetting some imbalance.

As she stared out the window, she spotted

a raven that took to the air. He became the fourth bird Ellie noticed on her second day of adventure. Somehow, she knew it was not Stone, but another raven who shared the land with her.

Ellie watched the unknown raven as he turned circles and flapped his wings in the afternoon sun.

Part of her wanted to roll down the window and call out to the bird in raven-speak. Instead, she watched him move across the sky. She studied how the sun shined off of his black wings.

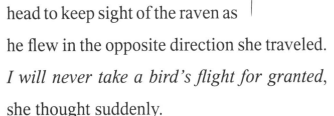

Ellie turned her head to keep sight of the raven as he flew in the opposite direction she traveled. *I will never take a bird's flight for granted,* she thought suddenly.

A few minutes later, Ellie arrived home.

Chapter Fifteen

Untangling

After a long bath, Ellie dried herself off with two towels. She put on her pajama bottoms and a clean T-shirt.

She used one of the towels to dry her hair. She continued to wring it and shake it until it was nearly dry. She grabbed her favorite brush from the drawer by the sink. She pulled her hair to one side. She brushed it in long, even strokes.

Brushing her hair brought Ellie a sense of calm. Somehow, all of the excitement of the day slipped off with each brushstroke.

Instead of rushing and frantically working out the knots, Ellie took her time to brush her hair and to get it untangled.

A few hours earlier, Ellie walked through the front door. Her grandmother let out a large sigh when she arrived.

"T'óó bíyó shi'diiłá nít'ę́ę́'," *I was starting to worry,* she said in Navajo. "You were gone quite awhile."

Without saying anything, Ellie moved close to her grandmother and gave her a big hug.

She whispered in her grandmother's ear, "Tsídii bich'į̄ yashti' nít'ę́ę́',"

I've been talking to the birds. I'm starting to learn.

Ellie pulled back. Her grandmother offered a small smile and nodded.

With Ellie's hair clean and dry, she returned to her grandmother, who sat in perfect quiet on the sofa. She had a plate of bread on the nearby table. Kyle went to their aunt and uncle's house, probably to use the computer. It left Ellie and her grandmother alone.

"T'ahdoo 'iish hxáshg'óó shitsii' shádiibish?" *Can you braid my hair for me before I go to bed?* Ellie asked.

Her grandmother gestured with both her hands for Ellie to sit. Ellie sat on the sofa with her back to her grandmother. She began to braid.

"T'áá 'íiyísí baahózhǫǫgo jíídą́ą́ ch'aanisíníyá," *I guess you had quite an adventure today,* her grandmother said in Navajo. She tugged at Ellie's hair and steadily twisted it. Ellie thought of her grandmother still as a weaver, as someone who pulls things together.

"I think so," Ellie said, speaking in Navajo.

"I just want you to be careful out there," her grandmother said. "Stay smart. Think. Use your judgment."

Ellie could not see it, but she knew her grandmother nodded firmly with each point.

She felt her grandmother quickly finish the end of her braid. Ellie pulled a hair tie off of her wrist and handed it to her grandmother. She secured the braid.

"K'ad," *There,* she said.

"Ahxé'hee'," *Thank you,* Ellie said.

She walked to her room and readied for bed.

Chapter Sixteen

It Begins

&llie woke suddenly. She felt a gentle shaking. Her grandmother's hands were on her shoulders.

"Élii, nídiidáh," *Wake up, Ellie,* her grandmother said in a soothing voice.

Ellie sat up in bed. She saw out of her window an early light in the eastern sky. The sun remained below the horizon. It was Monday.

"Ha'át'ííla'?" *What is it?* Ellie asked. She could have slept another half-hour before waking for school, she guessed.

"Someone is here to see you," her grandmother said calmly. "Outside."

"Ha'át'íí?" *What?* Ellie asked, confused

about who might visit her at home, so early in the morning.

Ellie followed her grandmother through the hallway, into the living room and to the front door. Her grandmother opened the door and stepped aside so her granddaughter could walk out.

In the weak light of morning, Ellie did not see anyone at first. She stepped through the door and outside into the cool air.

Ellie stopped.

Her body went rigid with shock.

From her driveway, out into the road and beyond the road, hundreds and hundreds of ravens stood side by side, in silence. Out in front, one large raven stood before all of them.

Ellie walked slowly to the one raven. She knew it to be Stone.

She kneeled down in front of Stone. She spoke in the raven's language, as quiet as she could, with clicks and small chirps. She did not want to wake her brother, aunt or uncle.

"What is this, Stone?" Ellie asked.

"What are all of these ravens doing here?"

She looked past Stone and wondered how many ravens stood behind him. Five hundred? One thousand?

"You said you were looking for knowledge," he said. "They have come, to bring it to you."

"All of them?" Ellie asked. She tried to keep her voice down, but she was overwhelmed.

"Turns out they have all been waiting for you," Stone said.

Then, he looked to the ground and looked back up at Ellie. "There's something you should know. Us ravens, along with some of the other birds, sent for the mockingbird. We sent for Wide-Sky. She traveled here to drop the manual before you. You were the one who would know how to use it."

"But the mockingbird returned," Ellie recalled, as she tried to make sense of everything. "She wanted the manual back."

"Actually, she just wanted to make sure you found it and tried it out," Stone responded.

He stepped closer. He added, "We have been waiting for the human who talks to birds."

Ellie looked down at her hands. They were shaking. A chill moved through her as she looked again to all of the ravens. They remained still and silent. Their eyes were focused on her.

Ellie looked back at them. She realized with each passing moment that something big was about to happen. It began as a small miracle and a few days of adventure, but much more was on the way.

"And so it begins," Stone said.

...to be continued

Acknowledgements

This book would not have been possible without the support and influence of many people. I have to extend many thanks to Sara Begay, a friend who taught me much about the Navajo culture. I also thank her mother, Bernice, who tried to teach me to speak at least some Navajo. During my time in Page, I also appreciated the interaction with the many students and faculty of the Page Unified School District. I learned about the world of Navajo youth through my time with them, as I covered the education beat for the newspaper.

I want to extend a fond appreciation to the staff of the Museum of Northern Arizona. The work they do to support the Navajo and Hopi cultures and share the knowledge with everyone is invaluable. My attendance of the summer festivals and events has furthered my understanding of our regional cultures — Navajo, Hopi and beyond.

When it comes to writing, I have to give proper credit to author and friend Mary Sojourner, who recognized that we shared the same problem: we're writers. She also mentored me through the rocky terrain of fiction. Along with Mary, my mom and dad always fostered my creativity. With their help, I found my path. They join my friends Megan Johnson and Ryan Hagerty in sharing my affinity for nature and earthly beauty.

The book would not be out in the world, either, if it were not for the staff of Salina Bookshelf. Despite the challenges of bringing this story to the page, they believed in both the story and in me. I owe them several cups of coffee and at least two lunches.

Finally, I extend all of the gratitude I could muster to my wife, Jane. She not only has been a huge supporter of me and a huge supporter of the book, she read the early chapters I wrote and said, "I need more." It was all I needed to keep going.

— Seth Muller

About the Author

Seth Muller was born and raised on the East Coast, but he truly fell in love with the Southwest. In early 2001, he moved to Page, Arizona. During his time there, he developed a fondness for the people and culture of the Navajo Nation. He currently lives with his wife Jane and daughter Grace in Flagstaff, Arizona, where he works as a magazine editor and contributor. He also wrote other books in the forthcoming Keepers of the Windclaw Chronicles.

About the Illustrator

Bahe Whitethorne, Jr. was born and raised in Flagstaff, AZ., and has been influenced in art by his father, Baje Whitethorne, Sr., a renowed Navajo artist. In 2002, he started working for Salina Bookshelf, Inc. and during that time, he helped develop Navajo Children's Picture Books. He has been working in Computer Graphics for six years, and only until 2008 has he begun an art career in painting. He currently lives in Flagstaff, Arizona.